SARAH'S WATERFALL

SARAH'S WATERFALL

*a healing story about
sexual abuse*

written by
ELLERY AKERS

illustrated by
ANGELIQUE BENICIO

The
SaferSociety
PRESS
BRANDON, VERMONT

Safer Society Press would like to thank Joanna Cotler, Ann Tobias, and Carol Chatsworth for their help with this book.

The purpose of this book is educational and informational in support of prevention, treatment, and therapy, and is not meant to replace conventional therapy. Readers should not rely upon it as recommending or promoting a specific method, diagnosis, or treatment for any particular situation. Specialists should be consulted where appropriate. Readers should evaluate all information and recommendations provided by organizations and Web sites cited or referred to in this work to determine its relevance to their particular situation. Internet Web sites listed in this work may have changed or disappeared between the time the work was written and when it is read. The author, reviewers, Safer Society Press, and Safer Society Foundation specifically disclaim all warranties, including without limitation any implied warranties of fitness for a particular purpose. No warranty is created or extended by any promotional statements made for this work.

Developmental Editor & Art Director: Gaen Murphree
Production Editor & Copy Editor: Collette Leonard
Book Designer: Peter Holm, Sterling Hill Productions
Compositor: Abrah Griggs, Sterling Hill Productions
Illustrator: Angelique Benicio
Proofreader: Susannah Noel

Printed in the United States of America
10 9 8 7 6 5 4 3 2 1

Library of Congress Cataloging-in-Publication Data
Akers, Ellery, 1946-
 Sarah's waterfall : a healing story about sexual abuse / Ellery Akers ; illustrated by Angelique Benicio. – 1st ed.
   p. cm.
 Summary: While attending a counseling group for sexually abused children, Sarah is asked to record her feelings in a journal.
 Includes bibliographical references (p.).
 ISBN 978-1-884444-79-1
 [1. Sexual abuse victims–Fiction. 2. Counseling–Fiction. 3. Diaries–Fiction.] I. Benicio, Angelique, ill. II. Title.
 PZ7.A305Sar 2009
 [Fic]–dc22

                    2008039408

PO Box 340
Brandon, Vermont 05733
www.safersociety.org
(802) 247-3132

Safer Society Press is a program of the Safer Society Foundation, a 501(c)3 nonprofit, dedicated to the prevention and treatment of sexual abuse. For more information, visit our Web site at www.safersociety.org.

Sarah's Waterfall: A Healing Story about Sexual Abuse
$16.95 plus shipping and handling
Order # WP135

This book is for
JACKIE DENNIS

Many thanks to
Rabia Mead, Padma Moyer, Marcia Anderson,
Latefa Mineo, Joanna Cotler, Susan Moon,
Bill Edmondson, Jerry Fleming, Judith Serin,
Barbara Bloom, and Deborah Reno.

Monday, August 23

My Journal

It's a little weird being in this after-school counseling group for sexually abused kids. But my Gram thinks it will help me. *Sexual abuse.* It sounds like measles. I like this journal they gave me, though. I like the sound of the crinkly, fancy paper when I turn the pages, and the swans on the cover, and the gold key. I keep the key around my neck on a silver chain. I like it that no one can ever open my journal but me. It's mine, and it's private. I guess I'm supposed to write and draw how I feel.

Okay. I feel dirty. Not just dirty. Yucky all over. Once I saw a car driving over a puddle, and mud splattered all over this fruit stand full of oranges and apples. All the apples got covered with mud. Yuck. They were so shiny and then they weren't. That's how I feel. Sometimes I just want to wash and wash and wash.

Monday, August 30

Gram

I live with my Gram. I used to visit her a lot, but now I live here all the time. She smells like lavender and she has big nighties and she has a real sponge that smells like the sea in her bathroom. She sings "Good morning, Merry Sunshine" to me every morning. Sometimes, when she does the laundry, she drops something on the floor, and she has a hard time picking it up, so she says, "Hand me that towel, Sarah, will you, darlin'. I'm just a fat old lady, can't hardly bend over anymore. Whoo-ee!"

At night I hear her drop to her knees beside her bed. Even though I'm in the next room, I know that *thunk* means she's dropped to the floor and is saying her

prayers. Then she pulls herself up, holding onto a bedpost and sighs, "Whoo-ee."

I feel better now that I'm not living with my stepdad. I got scared every time he passed my

2

door. I still have all my stuffed animals on my bed because sometimes it feels scary at night, but I tell them they're safe and they tell me I'm safe. And I feel safe with Gram.

Monday, September 6

Mrs. Bell's Group

Sometimes I feel like I'm bad all over and I smell bad. Once I was standing in assembly and it was so hot that I was sweating a lot and I had sweat under my arms and I was sure I stank. I was afraid people would notice, so I held my arms close to my body. And I feel *different.* But everybody in Mrs. Bell's group had the same thing happen to them. There're eight kids, all girls, and I'm getting to be

friends with Paula. The boys' group is across the hall. Mrs. Bell's the school psychologist. She's pretty nice.

Monday, September 20

Gram in the Morning

Sometimes when I come into Gram's room in the morning, she doesn't hear me because she's a little deaf. She sits on her bed in her nightie and tennis socks (she wears socks at night so her feet don't get cold). My bare feet on the floor don't make much noise, so she doesn't notice me at first. She sits with her head in her hands, and strands of gray hair stick out between her fingers. Her coffee pot bubbles and bubbles, and her coffee splats into the glass cap, and she looks tired. But then she looks up and sees me and says, "Good morning, darlin', you're up! Been up since four—I wake so early these days."

To make her laugh I say what they say in my French book, *"Ah, madame, bonjour!"* She laughs and says, "I'm glad to see you're learning your French!"

This morning, after breakfast, before Gram took me
to school, I told her sometimes I feel dirty and bad, and
she said, "Listen to me, darlin', there's nothing wrong
with you at all. You're good and you're beautiful. Your
momma's looking down on you from heaven, she's always
looking down on you, she loves you and she knows that's
true. There's not a speck of dirt on you, darlin'." Then
she took off her glass bead necklace and slipped it around
my neck. It felt cool on my collarbone, and pretty, and she

bent down and kissed the top of my head. She let me wear it all day.

Paula

Paula's not shy like me. She can tell jokes. ("What's red and yellow and red and yellow? An apple that works nights as a banana.") She has curly, bouncy hair (I wish I did) and when she calls me on the phone she says, "Yoo-hoo! It's me, Paula!" She's the only person I know who says "Yoo-hoo." She's smart, and she loves books like I do, and I showed her some of my poems and she liked them.

She has two dogs and a cat and a hamster, and she talks about her animals all the time. Every morning she taps each of her dogs on the nose with a Milk-Bone to give them a treat because she knows they'll miss her when she's at school. She says, "Be good, guys," and they snap up the Milk-Bones. I love going to Paula's. She has a whole bookcase full of books in her room. The first time

I went over, I felt so shy I started reading a book instead of talking to her, and I couldn't stop. I hurt her feelings and it was kind of rude, I guess, but I told her I was sorry, and it was okay. She gets crabby sometimes because she's so tired. She has nightmares almost every week about monsters or burglars climbing in the window, and she wakes up screaming and can't go back to sleep for a while. I have nightmares too, but not all the time.

Sunday, October 10

Going Out to Lunch with Gram

Gram took me to lunch this weekend and I had a hamburger on a bun with sesame seeds and I picked off a lot of the sesame seeds first. The napkins were made into little hats. Gram had soup and iced tea, and she sat back, wiped her mouth with the napkin, patted her stomach, and sighed, "Best thing I ever et!" She talks like that because she's from the South.

Sometimes I get embarrassed by the way she eats, just like a kid, sloppy, blowing on her soup and slurping it. But I love how she squeezes my hand when we're eating and says, "Just had a wave of love for you, darlin'."

I love her purse with the tortoiseshell clasps she snaps closed with a sigh when she's tired. She loves to eat and she loves to do collage—she's a collage artist. That means cutting up pictures from magazines and gluing them all together to make a new picture. She loves to play canasta with her friend Alma and she loves poetry, like me. She's always breaking into poetry. Every once in a while, when she drops me at school, she blows me a kiss and says, "'Parting is such sweet sorrow.' That's poetry, darlin', from a play. WILLIAM SHAKESPEARE."

Paula and I Make Up Words

Paula and I are making up words and what they mean.

To spirgle: to sneak sugar packets out of the bowl at lunch and let them melt on your tongue.

Frizzshooflia: really curly hair. (Paula has frizzshooflia.)

To mizle: to be mean to a kid and make them feel embarrassed. Sometimes grownups are mizlers. That's what I think.

Saffoling: walking in the rain in your nightie. (That was Paula's idea from when she went to camp last summer.)

Saturday, October 16

Gram Takes Paula and Me to the Natural History Museum

Gram and Paula and I went to the aquarium and looked at the fish, all colors. Paula went from exhibit to exhibit, tapping on the glass and talking to everybody, but Gram and I sat in front of one of the tanks of angelfish and she said, "How beautiful, how beautiful. Those fish look just like flowers underwater. Whoever invented the aquarium, I take my hat off to him."

Then we went outside to the herb garden, and they let us pick the plants. We picked basil and rosemary and sage and lavender and we took them to Gram, and she kept smelling them for a long time, holding the sprigs of plants between her thumb and forefinger and saying, "Paula, that one's marvelous! Darlin', that's wonderful!" Finally she said, "I'll press 'em, darlin', and smell 'em later," and she folded them in a bit of paper and put them in her purse with the big tortoiseshell clasps and snapped it shut.

Then she took us out to lunch at that café with the

napkins in little hats. Paula showed me her box of
spesshies. That's where she keeps special things, all small,
like a tiny pad and pencil and a shiny pebble. She was
glad we went to the museum because she bought a little
starfish to add to her collection.

Monday, October 18

Paula

I asked Paula if she ever feels like she spaces out and drifts away in the air. She says she does, and Mrs. Bell told her lots of kids who were sexually abused do that. Lots of us spend time in the sky, and it's okay. That made me feel better, like I wasn't alone. "There's nothing wrong with you, Sarah," Paula said. "There's nothing wrong with you, either," I said.

Here's a poem I wrote for Paula:

To Paula, My Best Friend

Before I met you
I had a best friend, Shirley
She told me I was a good kid
and pretty
but she was imaginary

But now I have you
with your freckles and striped socks
and your frizzshooflia
Sometimes we fight and make up
but you're real
and you have dogs, too

Molly flops down *beside* me when I'm sad
Frankie jumps up when I come in
Since I met you
I don't spend so much time in the air

I showed it to Paula and she really liked it. Then we both wrote a solemn declaration of the Anti-P.E. Club. She doesn't like to hang by those rings and I don't like those sawhorses, and I feel shy changing into my gym clothes with all those lockers clanging closed around me and kids yelling. I always go past the right number on my combination lock and have to go back. Besides, my gym shoes always smell damp. We both wish we could go to the library instead of P.E.

Monday, October 25

Mrs. Bell's Assignment

I really like Mrs. Bell. She's different from the teachers at school. Miss Barrows wears clunky black shoes and

Miss Barrows Mrs. Bell Miss Wainwright

high collars and shushes Paula in class and Miss Wainwright in gym is tall and skinny like a flagpole and is always blowing that whistle, but Mrs. Bell seems happy and likes us a lot. She just got married, and she always wears perfume. We draw a lot and she puts on music to help us draw. She says kids sometimes feel dirty when somebody older touches their private places, but it's never the kids' fault. The kid is *not* bad. The kid is *not* dirty. The kid is *clean.*

She wants us to draw what feeling clean looks like. Some kids are drawing taking a bath, but I want to draw taking a shower. The summer before last, Gram and I took a trip out West to Yosemite in the Sierra mountains, and we saw a waterfall called Bridalveil. All this beautiful white water poured down and it sounded a hundred times louder than a shower and it smelled fresh and it sparkled. I loved it. So I'm going to draw standing under that waterfall and spinning around so every last bit of dirt I feel gets washed off. I'm going to draw that waterfall and that moss and all those flowers, and then I'm going to draw the clothes I'm going to put on afterward.

Saturday, October 30
Drawing in Gram's Studio

I had a cold this weekend so I stayed in Gram's studio, sniffling and drawing, while she was working on her collage. She's going to help me with my assignment and cut out pictures of pretty soaps and flowers so I can paste them on my drawing.

We sat there for hours, me with my Kleenexes and crayons, and Gram humming and singing to herself and cutting out pictures.

"Oh, darlin'," she said, "I wish I could have that mean old cold for you. Just bring me that Dog drawer, would you?" She's got a cabinet with little drawers with different labels, like Dogs, Rivers, Horses, Flowers, and Fish.

I brought her the Dog drawer and she picked through it to find just the right kind of dog for her collage. Gram has arthritis, so her knuckles are knob-bly, but she doesn't seem to have trou-ble cutting out a spaniel's tail or the fringes of a leaf with those tiny nail scissors.

She doesn't always get dressed when she's in her studio, and this weekend we were both in our nighties. She has these bright pink high-heeled slippers with pom-poms and when she gets up to look through her magazine piles they go *clop, clop.*

Gram never rushes her artwork. She cut out a begonia so carefully—a big one—and then lifted it gently onto the paper with her scissors. First she tried putting it in the sky so it was floating over a lake. Then she put it in the lake. All the time she was twirling her round tortoiseshell glasses that make her look like an owl when she wears them.

Then she put the begonia on the ground and a dog racing across the sky and said, "That's it, darlin'. My picture's finished."

She went into the kitchen and started making chicken soup and hot lemonade for my cold. I was feeling a lot better. So as I listened to her chopping carrots, I started making her a paper dinner. I haven't made one since I was a little kid. First I drew a salad, baked potatoes, and chocolate cake, her favorite. Then I cut them all out and put them on a tray and I walked into the kitchen with a towel over my arm like a real waiter in a fancy restaurant. "Whoo-ee, darlin', look at you!" said Gram. She pretended to eat everything and rolled her eyes and said it was delicious. I ran into the other room and cut out another square and crayoned it yellow for more butter, and she said, "Butter, darlin', and baked potatoes! My favorite! You know I love butter and baked potatoes."

Here's my drawing for Mrs. Bell:

Wonder Woman

My stuffed animals, Angelique, Margo, and Tumba getting clean, too.

Pretty soaps

Here I am, standing under the waterfall and all that mud I felt on top of me is washing away. Mrs. Bell said I could put anybody in the picture I wanted to help me, so I put in Wonder Woman washing my hair and I'm spinning and dancing out of there and the water smells fresh and is pouring all over me and I'm feeling really CLEAN. I'M BEAUTIFUL, INSIDE AND OUT.

eagle wings to fly around with ↓

Here I am in my *beautiful clean clothes:* ↓

Here's my beautiful clean body—I put on some of that shimmering paint Mrs. Bell gave us, and I'm shining all over. ↓

a blue dress with long sleeves made of stars ↘

a glass bead necklace, like Gram's ↖

Here's a soft white towel all ready for me and Wonder Woman wraps me in it. ↖

soft moccasins ↖

I didn't do anything bad. Mrs. Bell says that anybody who touches kids and makes them feel scared like that is always wrong. *He* was bad, not me. And all that mud belongs to him, not me. He dumped it on me, yuck, but I get to dump it back on him. Here he is all covered with icky icky mud on *him*, not *me*. It's his mud, not mine. *He's* the dirty one.

Monday, November 1

Paula and I Show Each Other Our Pictures

I showed Paula my picture, and she really liked it.

She showed me hers. In her picture, she was taking a bath, and on the bathroom door was a big sign saying KEEP OUT! PRIVATE! GUARD DOGS! BEWARE! Both her dogs were protecting her and growling, even her golden retriever, Molly, who never even barks at the

mailman. And she looked happy standing in the tub, and she put, "I'M CLEAN! I WAS ALWAYS CLEAN!" And her dogs were saying, "Go, Girl!" Her cat was curled up on the bath mat, and Hammy the Hamster was holding up a sign saying, "Paula's great!"

Friday, November 12
Feeling Sad Again

This afternoon I was reading in bed with my library books scattered over my blue quilt, and I kept remembering all that scary stuff, and I couldn't stop crying.

Gram must have heard me and she came into the room and sat beside me on the bed and said, "Oh, darlin'."

"Why'd it have to happen?" I asked.

"Oh, darlin', I'm so sorry. But I'm glad you told. You know I'd do anything for you. If I could go back in time and keep it from happening, I'd walk all over the world, and cross jungles, and climb mountains, and swim across the Atlantic, and even the Pacific. We'll get through this together, darlin'."

After a while, when I was hiccuping from crying so hard and even my ears were wet, she patted me on the back and said, "I know what we should do, darlin'. Let's go plant some basil in a pot and put it in the kitchen window. By the time it comes up, you'll feel a lot better, I know you will."

So we got out the seed packets and I put some basil seeds in a pot and watered them. I was so tired from crying, I went to bed early, but it was a good kind of tired.

Playing Cards with Gram

Today I played canasta with Gram. We sat all afternoon on her flowered sofa with the card table in front of us.

I loved shuffling the cards and listening to them snap as I splatted them back and forth. When I dealt, I counted under my breath as the cards fanned out.

Gram scooped hers up all at once and sighed with disappointment. "Oh, what a hand! Not what I wanted. I like it not! I like it not!"

I won. I usually win because I'm careful and Gram gambles everything on a single card. She laughed when she lost and threw up her hands. "Oh, you've got me! You've got me, darlin'! 900 points!"

Sometimes when she picks up a good card from the deck, like a joker, she shows it to me: "A joker! How about that!" You're not supposed to show the other player your cards, but Gram does.

I chew my braids when I'm deciding what card to put down, but Gram never tells me to stop like Miss Barrows, the geography teacher, does at school. Gram just laughs and says, "Don't worry, darlin', win or lose, 'sunshine follows the rain,' as the poet said." Then she squeezes my hand.

Monday, December 6
Exercises

Mrs. Bell had us do some body exercises today. At first, Paula and I looked at each other and whispered "Yuck!" But it wasn't like P.E. at all, it was fun.

"Okay, everybody," said Mrs. Bell, "take a deep breath. Now pretend you're an oak tree. Raise your arms like they were branches, and feel as if you're touching the sky. Now feel your feet are strong roots that go through the floor and way down into the ground."

I looked over at Paula: she looked strong and solid, and was breathing deeply. I thought how tree roots go deep in the dark earth, past the stones, and sink down, and my feet felt heavy.

"Great!" said Mrs. Bell, after a while. "Now stomp around a little." We stomped for a while, and that was fun.

"Now everybody hum." I chanted *Hmmmmm* deep in my chest, and it felt good. Once last year I tiptoed into the music room and lifted the piano lid and touched the metal strings and it vibrated all through me and went on echoing through the room: it was just like that.

"You're all humming wonderfully. And now, take a deep breath and say *Voooooo*," Mrs. Bell said. We all said *Voooooo*. It made me giggle; it sounded like French class.

"The last thing we're going to do is yawn," Mrs. Bell said. "You know, like a cat or a dog when it stretches."

"Paula," I said, as we yawned, "you look just like Molly when she gets up from a nap!"

"Good," she said. "I think golden retrievers are just as beautiful as people. Maybe more beautiful. You know what Molly keeps doing? She keeps eating Frankie's food. I have to feed her separately. Want to come over after and help feed the mules?"

She calls her animals "the mules."

"Sure," I said, "I'll call Gram. I love feeding your mules."

I had a great time at Paula's, and when I got home, I put my waterfall drawing on the wall next to my bed: I want to look at it before I go to sleep.

Monday, December 13

Gram's Coat Lining

I was so cold walking back from the bus today. My feet were icy inside my galoshes, and every time I came to a street corner, I got blasted by the wind. I told Gram how cold I was when I got home.

"We could go shopping tomorrow after school and get you a new coat."

"But I like that coat. It has flowers on it."

"Okay, darlin', I'll fix it."

So she got out some scissors and went to her closet and cut out the fluffy lining in her best coat and cut it to my size. Then she got out a needle and thread and sewed her lining into my coat, humming a little. "There, darlin'. You'll have that inside your coat and you won't be cold." Now I don't mind the wind at all. I love Gram.

Saturday, January 1
New Year's Day

I walked into Gram's room this morning and she broke into poetry like she does sometimes: "'Ring out, wild bells! Ring out the old, ring in the new!' TENNYSON, darlin'."

"How do you know so much poetry, Gram?" I said.

"Well, I don't know if I ever told you this story before, Sarah. I keep forgetting what I've already said because when people get old, they're apt to go a bit gaga. Did I ever tell you about reciting poetry for my grandfather?"

"No, Gram."

"Well, my grandfather loved hearing poetry and he used to take me downtown to where all his cronies sat around in the park, and I stood on a bench and recited poetry to all his friends. I loved it. Sometimes I think people in my time were better off than they are now, and happier. It's a different world, Sarah, a different world."

She shook her head and looked at the photo of my grandpa, her husband, who I never knew. He died before I was born.

"No one remembers my Jack, but I do." She looked sad for a minute. Then she smiled and hugged me.

"It's a grand life, if you don't weaken. Well now, how about pancakes for the New Year?"

So we made ourselves pancakes with butter and maple syrup and they were almost an inch thick.

I did a new water- fall drawing for the New Year.

Here I am, flying around, all sparkly, in my star dress, with my eagle wings. Wonder Woman and bluebirds and butterflies are flying with me.

Here's the spray from the waterfall, and all the mosses and ferns, though I had a hard time drawing them—they look a little clunky.

Tonight I checked on the pot in the kitchen window and the basil had leaves big enough to pick, so I picked some, and Gram and I made spaghetti sauce, and it was really good.

Monday, January 10
Jell-O and a Safe Place Day

We walked into Mrs. Bell's group today and she had daisies in pots along the wall and a couple of plates of Jell-O on the table. Chris went right up and poked one of the blocks of lime Jell-O and it quivered and shook, and she started to laugh.

"Chris!" one of the kids behind me said, shocked, but Mrs. Bell said it was okay, and we watched the Jell-O wobble.

"Okay, everybody," she said, "I want you to shake like a big plate of Jell-O. So take a deep breath, and jiggle all over like Jell-O. Whatever you feel, it's okay. If you feel sad

or mad, that's okay. Just let the shaking happen. I'll be right here if you need me."

So I took a deep breath, and started to shake just like Jell-O, and it made me feel tingly and at first my stomach felt tight, and then it felt warm afterward, and I started to giggle.

Paula was crying, though, and Mrs. Bell patted her on the back.

I looked around the room and the daisies looked beautiful and I noticed some dust specks drifting through a

ray of light that fell on the floor. Each one flashed like a spark lit up in the sun, then it went dull again. I felt calm.

"That was great, everybody! You all looked just like Jell-O! Good for you. Now take out your journals and draw a safe place and a comfy chair and anything special that makes you feel comforted and safe—maybe a photograph, a stuffed animal, a person, or a dog."

I smiled at Paula. She was red-eyed, but she didn't look sad anymore—I knew she was going to put in all her dogs, her cat, and Hammy the Hamster.

I drew myself sitting on Gram's flowered sofa, and my poems were right next to me, and Paula's dog Molly was lying beside me, and Gram had her hand on my shoulder.

I could almost feel myself sinking into that sofa, my back resting against it, and my stomach felt warm as I looked at my picture, and my feet felt comfy, just like they were resting in my polka-dotted slippers on Gram's hooked rug.

"Sarah, I put you in my drawing, and my box of spesshies, and all my animals," said Paula.

"I drew Molly."

"She loves you, Sarah. She always lies down next to you when you come over. She never did that for anybody else."

Monday, January 17
Rivera's Florist

This afternoon the bus was so late I got cold, even with Gram's coat lining. For a while I stood on top of a heating vent on the street, but finally I went into Rivera's Florist, where it was warm.

Every time Mrs. Rivera opened the glass case of flowers, the smell of lilies and green things drifted into the room, and it smelled like spring. She put a basket of mosses and ferns on the counter, and they looked just like the ones at Bridalveil, so I took out my journal and started to draw.

I didn't think Mrs. Rivera was noticing, but she came over and said, "Are you an artist, sweetheart?"

I felt so shy I didn't know what to say.

"Not really. I write poems sometimes."

"Drawing and writing," she said, "That's great, sweetheart." And she gave me some ferns to take home.

This is my third waterfall drawing. It makes me want to go back to Yosemite, and lie on one of those big granite boulders in the warm sun, and stare at the clouds with Gram, like we did the summer before last.

Saturday, January 24

Glasses

For months now I've been squinting on the bus, trying to look out the window at street signs, but they've been getting blurrier. So I told Gram and she took me to an eye doctor to get my eyes tested, and today I got glasses. I was so surprised when I put them on and we walked down the street. The corners of buildings are so pointed! I could even see needles on the tops of fir trees in the park. And the stars at night aren't fuzzy at all—they're sharp as nails.

Monday, February 7

Paula and I Nap with Her Dogs

Mrs. Bell told Paula and me to go right up to Paula's dogs and feel the way they breathe. So we went to Paula's house: she let herself in with her key—her mom works late. Frankie and Molly were sleeping by the radiator.

Paula snuggled up to Frankie, her beagle, and laid her head on his chest, and listened to his heartbeat.

"You old snoozer," she said, patting him. "Yoo-hoo." But he didn't wake up. He just snorted.

I lay on the rug with my hand on Molly and felt her

chest rise and fall. Every time she breathed out, the license on her collar clinked a little.

"Do you think they're dreaming, Paula?"

"Maybe. Sometimes Frankie's paws twitch and it looks like he's chasing rabbits. Nobody knows."

"Do you still get nightmares, Paula?"

"Yeah, but it's better. I don't get them all the time, like before."

"That's good."

We lay there for a while listening to Molly and Frankie breathing, and then we fell asleep on the rug.

Monday, February 21
Circle Talk

Today we went around in the group and said how we feel.

"Anything good happen this week? Any scary things?" said Mrs. Bell. "Anybody have a chance to practice some of the exercises?"

I was glad I didn't have to go first.

"My mom yelled at me. Sometimes I just *hate* my mom,"
Chris burst out. "I just want to hit her and kick her."

"It's okay to feel that way," said Mrs. Bell. "Remember, it
happened to me too, when I was your age, and I was mad
at my mom for not protecting me. You know what helped
me? Throwing pillows and stomping around. Have you
got any pillows you could throw?"

"Yeah," said Chris, "I got lots."

"I used to think I was crazy before I came here," said
Kim. "My cousin was cool, he was 15, he used to help me
with my math homework, and I thought he was really

nice. Then when he started acting different, I felt really mixed up."

"It's hard when someone you care about starts touching you and you know it's not okay," said Mrs. Bell.

"Yeah," said Keisha, "I felt really weird. It was awful."

"It's confusing," added Mrs. Bell, "but it's okay to feel mad at someone and still like other things about them."

"I used to be scared all the time and get stomach aches," said Maria, "and now I'm hardly ever scared, but last night when I was watching TV I got scared again."

"I'm glad you feel better most of the time," said Mrs. Bell. "Once in a while you might get scared again. But the scary feelings go away after a while. It just takes time."

"I'm sleeping better!" said Paula.

"Great!"

"I have a new waterfall drawing," I said.

"Terrific. How many is that now, Sarah?"

"It's my third one," I said. "I look at them next to my bed before I go to sleep."

Paula Teaches Geography Class

Miss Barrows caught Paula talking in geography today and she must have been in a bad mood because she said, "All right, Paula, if you want to talk so much, why don't you come up here and *you* teach the class."

It got quiet in the room. Somebody got up and sharpened a pencil, and the kid behind me snapped her binder shut with a click.

Paula looked nervous and I started to yawn and hum under my breath and whispered to her, "Oak tree." She went to the blackboard, and stood with her back to the class. I knew she was humming and yawning, and then pretending to be an oak tree, with her feet like roots in the ground, but nobody else did. When she turned around, she was holding a piece of chalk and grinning. She started drawing a map on the board.

"This is the kingdom of Frizzshooflia," she said, "and the Frizzshooflians go down to this river" (she drew a

squiggly line), "which borders the country of Chocolatia, where everybody eats chocolate all the time."

"Hey, I want to go there," said one kid, and then everybody started to laugh. Miss Barrows pursed her lips and said, "All right, Paula, very funny. You can sit down, now."

After class I went up to Paula and said, "You were great."

"Thanks for reminding me about that stuff," she said. "It really helped. I felt I could do anything. I kind of *like* teaching!"

Mrs. Bell

I really love Mrs. Bell. I was sitting three seats behind
her on the bus, and I could see her purple scarf thrown
over her shoulder, but she didn't see me. Today I showed
her one of my poems and she said it was WONDERFUL
and LOVELY. She writes poems, too! She asked me how
I decided to end my poem, and she said she always has
trouble ending her poems. She's been published in magazines. A real writer likes my poems! She says she'll bring
some of hers to show me. I watched her get off at her bus
stop and I waved at her out the window, but I don't think
she saw me. I watched her walk all the way up the street.
She walks gracefully, even in the snow in her galoshes, like
she's floating. I like it that she's quiet, like me.

Here's the poem I showed her:

Sometimes, When I'm Scared

Sometimes when I'm awake at night
and Gram's snoring
and I don't want to wake her up

Sometimes when she doesn't know how scared I am
or seems too tired

I look at my waterfall drawings
I hold myself in my own arms
I hum to myself
and rock back and forth
and I feel safe

Thursday, March 10

I Feel Like Wonder Woman

Today at recess Butch Follett almost knocked me down.
He was in a hurry, and he pushed me, and I was so startled
I almost fell in a puddle. I ran into the bathroom, and
Paula ran in after me.

I started to cry, and she put her hand on my shoulder
and said, "Hey, Sarah, what about that Jell-O exercise!"

Then we both pretended we were Jell-O, and I shook
and shook, and Paula gave me a hug.

"That Butch makes me so mad," I said.

"That Butch is gross," said Paula, and she pretended to
throw up.

"That Butch is so BLECH!" she said. "YECH! BLECH!" By this time we were shouting YUCK YECH BLECH and stomping around the bathroom. I stomped on some paper towels on the floor and my legs felt strong and I started to giggle.

That afternoon I went up to Butch before English class and I told him I didn't like it when he pushed me, and he looked surprised and said he was sorry. I felt like Wonder Woman with her zinc bracelets, talking to him like that. I felt strong.

Sunday, April 10

My Birthday

I woke up hearing the sprinkler sputter in the yard, and I knew Gram was gardening. Then I remembered my last birthday, when I was so scared I used to fold myself as small as I could in bed. It seems like a long time ago. I'm glad I told. I hated keeping that secret.

Gram came in, singing "Happy Birthday" instead of "Good Morning, Merry Sunshine" like she usually does. She was wearing her striped spring dress and one of those party favor hats, and she tooted on a toy trumpet.

"Paula's called twice already, darlin', before you woke up. What do you want to do today?"

"Let's have breakfast on the porch."

So we had scrambled eggs and toast on that little rickety iron table, and a sparrow hopped down next to me, looking for crumbs. Gram brought me a cup with chocolate icing from my cake. We rocked back and forth on the porch swing, though it was a little rusty from the winter, and sat on those poofy plastic cushions that sigh when you sit down, and I ate the icing slowly. It was really good.

We had a great party at lunch, with balloons. Gram gave me a birthday card that said, "I'm so proud of you, darlin'." She also gave me one of her favorite books of poems. She marked a poem in the book that said, "She walks in beauty, like the night, of cloudless climes and starry skies." And she wrote on the bookmark, "That's you, darlin'. You walk in beauty."

Paula gave me a notebook with daffodils on the cover, to write poems in. And a card that said, "For my best friend, Sarah, THE AUTHOR!!!!

"P.S. And DRAWER!!!!

"P.S.S. I mean *artist*!!!! Drawer sounds like a cabinet or something.

"P.S.S.S. How do you get six elephants in a Volkswagen? Three in the front and three in the back! Ha, Ha."

Monday, April 11

Ten Things That Make Me Happy

Today in Mrs. Bell's group we're writing a list of ten things that make us happy. So here's mine:

1. Gram blowing a kiss out the car window when she drops me at school

2. making cinnamon toast with Paula

3. the smell of pink erasers

4. my waterfall drawings

5. the sound of Gram shuffling papers in her studio and humming to herself

6. opening a tangerine and eating it

7. watering Gram's roses in the yard and smelling the wet earth as the hose splatters across their leaves

8. feeling safe, like I used to before it happened

9. Mrs. Bell asking to see more of my poems

10. goofing around with my birthday balloons as they drift up to the ceiling and squeak and drift down again

Paula and I Are Going to Yosemite

Paula and I started talking after Mrs. Bell's group, and we agreed that neither of us is dirty, and none of the other kids are, either. I know what happened to her was not her fault, and she said the same to me. I know it's true for her, so it must be true for me. Sometimes kids just have bad luck, that's all, like when I had the flu for three weeks. And sometimes grownups or older kids do mean things. I feel better now. I don't feel so scared, and I don't feel alone. If I ever met another kid who got touched in their private places by somebody older, I'd tell them it was *not their fault,* and not to be ashamed.

Gram's taking Paula and me to Yosemite this summer, and she's promised to make pancakes every morning. I can't wait to show Paula all that white granite you can see flashing through the woods from a distance—then you know you're in the Sierras. I can't wait to go for a hike with her and smell the pine needles on the ground in the sun and listen to the rush of water that used to be snow.

We're all going to hike up to Bridalveil—we'll go slow for Gram. We're going to listen to that water pour and watch the wind lift the spray as it floats down and sparkles. I'm going to stand there and sniff the mist and look at all those ferns and mosses. I'm going to take my journal and draw my last waterfall drawing there. I don't think I need them anymore. I feel clean.

ACKNOWLEDGMENTS

Except for the "Drawing Feeling Clean" and "Throwing the Pillow" assignments, all the body exercises taught by "Mrs. Bell" were developed by pioneering somatic psychologists Julie Henderson and Peter A. Levine or by family and child therapist Maggie Kline. I've found their books and audio format CDs to be an important healing resource.

I'm grateful to Julie Henderson for her yawning, humming, rocking, stomping, and "playful retching" exercises recounted in her book, *Embodying Well Being: or How to Feel as Good as You Can in Spite of Everything* (Julie Henderson, Zapchen Somatics, 2003). To learn more about Julie Henderson's work, go to www.zapchen.com.

I'm grateful to Peter A. Levine and Maggie Kline for their exercises described in their books. The "Magic in Me/Oak Tree" and "Bowl of Jell-O" exercises by Peter A. Levine and Maggie Kline, are adapted from their books, *Trauma Through a Child's Eyes: Awakening the Ordinary Miracle of Healing* (Peter A. Levine and Maggie Kline, North Atlantic Books, 2007) and *Trauma-Proofing Your Kids* (Peter A. Levine and Maggie Kline, North Atlantic Books, 2008) and also appear in the audio format CD *Parent's Guide to It Won't Hurt Forever: Guiding Your Child Through Trauma* (Peter A. Levine, Sounds True, 2005). The "Voooooo" exercise and "Drawing a Safe Place" exercise are adapted from the audio format CD *Sexual Healing: Transforming the Sacred Wound* (Peter A. Levine, Sounds True, 2003). "Paula and I Nap With Her Dogs" is adapted from the "Animal" exercise in the book, *Healing Trauma: A Pioneering Program for Restoring the Wisdom of Your Body* (Peter A. Levine, Sounds True, 2005). Other ideas about healing that have influenced the story appear in *Waking the Tiger: Healing Trauma* (Peter A. Levine and Ann Frederick, North Atlantic Books, 1997). To contact Peter A. Levine or to find a Somatic Experiencing® practitioner, go to www.traumahealing.com.

I'm also indebted to ideas from two insightful books, *Helping Your Child Recover from Sexual Abuse* (Caren Adams and Jennifer Fay, University of Washington Press, 2003) and *Strong at the Heart: How It Feels to Heal from Sexual Abuse* (Carolyn Lehman, Farrar, Straus and Giroux, 2005).

HELP FOR KIDS

If you're a kid who's been sexually abused, you can call these numbers anytime, *day or night,* and talk to a counselor who will listen to you and help. It's free. And no one knows who you are.

1-800-422-4453 (1-800-4-A-CHILD)

When the recording answers, press 1 to speak to a counselor.

Childhelp National Child Abuse Hotline

Childhelp, www.childhelp.org

In Canada, you can call Kids Help Phone, 1-800-668-6868 (www.kidshelpphone.ca).

Please remember . . .

- You're not alone. This has happened to a lot of kids. Look at Sarah and Paula and how they eventually felt better.

- It wasn't your fault. You weren't to blame. When a child is sexually abused by someone older, the older person is *always* responsible, no matter what the kid did or didn't do.

- If you are still dealing with this alone, reach out to a relative, friend, teacher, or counselor to get the help you need and tell them what happened. Keep telling until someone listens to you and helps you.

- All your feelings are okay. Sexually abused kids can often feel sad, angry, numb, scared, confused—or can have a lot of other feelings too.

ABOUT THE AUTHOR

Ellery Akers is a writer, artist, and naturalist living on the coast of Northern California. She received a B.A. from Harvard and an M.A. from San Francisco State University.

Her collection of poems, *Knocking on the Earth,* from Wesleyan University Press (1989), was named one of the year's best books by the *San Jose Mercury News.* She has won six national awards for writing, including the John Masefield Award, the Paumanok Award, and *Sierra* magazine's Nature Writing Award. Her poetry has been featured on National Public Radio and has appeared in *The American Poetry Review, Harvard, The Sun,* and many other magazines. Her nature essays have been published in numerous magazines and anthologies, and her play, *Letters to Anna, 1846–54,* won a Dominican University One Act Play Festival Award in 2003.

A sexual abuse survivor herself, Ellery has long been interested in creativity as a tool for healing and has taught poetry workshops for both children and adults. She as taught writing at Cabrillo College and has led natural history field trips for the Audubon Society, the College of Marin, and San Francisco State University.

An award-winning visual artist as well, Ellery has exhibited her artwork in many galleries and museums nationally.

ABOUT THE ILLUSTRATOR

Angelique Benicio was born in 1962 in Cromwell, Connecticut, one of five creative children to her artistic parents. She pursued a formal education in fine art at San Jose State University, California, and then moved to Marin County where for twelve years she painted, sculpted, and worked as an illustrator and graphic artist. She traveled in Brazil from 1992 to 1994 creating hand-sculpted dolls and writing short stories for children. It was during this period that she discovered her love of creating art with a child's perspective as inspiration. On her return to the U.S. she began to explore the children's market, creating illustration for puzzles, games, and poster art.

In 2002 Angelique moved to Paris, France, working for five years as a painter and sculptor in cinema special effects and working as an illustrator for children's magazines. She currently lives in Rio de Janeiro, Brazil, with her husband and two children. Her energies continue to be focused on family, art, and telling stories with pictures.